This book belongs to:

....

First American edition, 1987.
Text and illustrations copyright © 1987 by Jill Murphy.
All rights reserved.
Originated and published in Great Britain by Walker Books Ltd., 1987.
Printed and bound in Italy.
Library of Congress Cataloging-in-Publication Data
Murphy, Jill. All in one piece.
Summary: Four young elephants help their
parents get ready to go to a dinner-dance.
[1. Family life — Fiction. 2. Elephants — Fiction] I. Title.
PZ7.M9534A1   1987   [E]   87-2516
ISBN 0-399-21433-X
First impression

All in One Piece

Jill Murphy

G.P. Putnam's Sons
New York

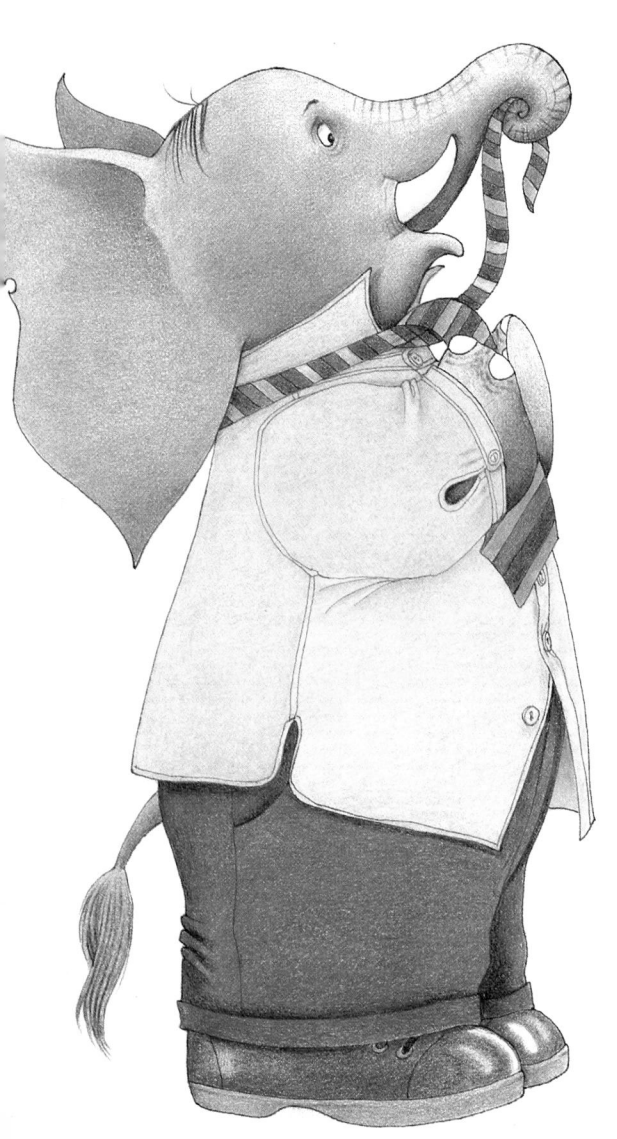

Mr. Large was getting ready for work.
"Don't forget the office dinner dance
tonight, dear," he said.
"Of course I won't," said Mrs. Large.
"I've been thinking about it all year."

"Are children allowed at the dinner dance?"
  asked Lester.

"No," said Mrs. Large. "It'll be too late
  for little ones."

"What about the baby?" asked Luke.

"Granny is coming to take care of everyone,"
  said Mrs. Large, "so there's no need to worry."

Granny arrived at supper time. The children were already bathed and in their pajamas. Granny gave them some painting to do while she tidied up and Mr. and Mrs. Large went upstairs to get ready.

Luke sneaked into the bathroom while
Mr. Large was shaving.
"Will I have to shave when I grow up?"
he asked, patting foam onto his trunk.
"Go away," said Mr. Large. "I don't want
you ruining my best trousers!"

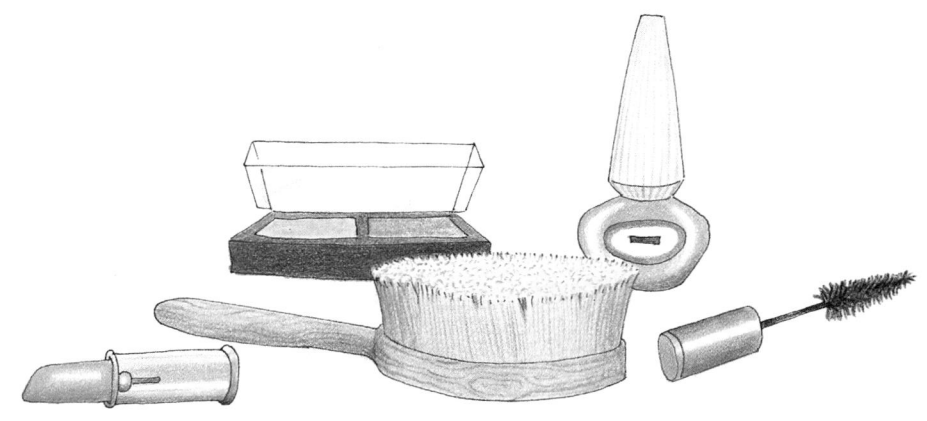

The baby crept into the bedroom where
Mrs. Large was putting on her make up.
Mrs. Large didn't notice until it was too late.

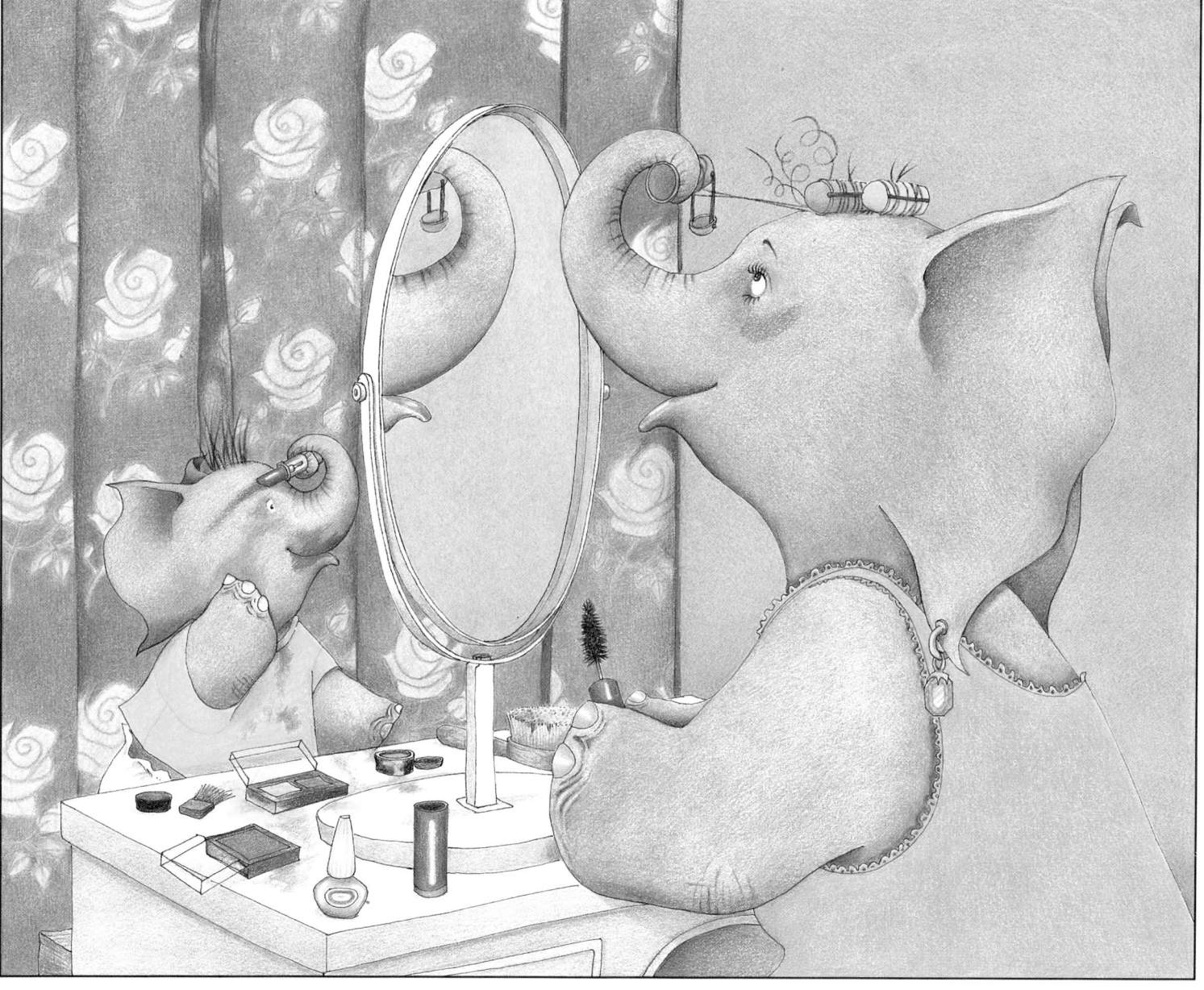

"Look!" said the baby. "Pretty!"

"Don't move," said Mrs. Large. "Don't
touch *anything*!"

Outside on the landing, things were
even worse. Laura was clopping about in
her mother's best shoes and beads, and
Lester and Luke were seeing how many
toys they could cram into her new tights.

"Downstairs at *once*!" bellowed Mrs. Large.
"Can't I have just one night in the whole year
to myself? One night when I am not covered in
jam and poster paint? One night when I can put
on my new dress and walk through the front
door all in one piece?"

The children went downstairs to Granny.
Mr. Large followed soon after, very handsome
in his best suit. At last, Mrs. Large
appeared in the doorway.
"How do I look?" she asked.

"Pretty, Mommy!" gasped the children.

"You look smashing!" said Mr. Large.

"Just like a movie star, dear,"
  said Granny.

"Hands off!" said Mrs. Large to the
  paint-smeared children.

Mr. and Mrs. Large got ready to leave.

"Goodbye everyone," they said. "Be good now."

The baby began to cry.

"Just go," said Granny, picking her up.

"She'll stop as soon as you've left. Have a
lovely time."

"We've escaped," said Mr. Large with a smile,
closing the front door behind them.
"All in one piece," said Mrs. Large, "and
not a smear of paint between us."
"Actually," said Mr. Large gallantly, "you'd
look wonderful to me, even if you were
covered in paint."

Which was perfectly true …
and just as well really!